For Jill and Karen
MM

For Darya, for teaching me how to play again
RJB

Library of Congress Cataloging-in-Publication data is on file with the publisher.

Text copyright © 2019 by Maryann Macdonald
Illustrations copyright © 2019 by Rahele Jomepour Bell
First published in the United States of America in 2019 by Albert Whitman & Company
ISBN 978-0-8075-6552-0

Printed in China
10 9 8 7 6 5 4 3 2 1 WKT 22 21 20 19 18

Design by Rick DeMonico

For more information about Albert Whitman & Company,
visit our website at www.albertwhitman.com.

100 years of Albert Whitman & Company
Celebrate with us in 2019!

PLAYDATE

Maryann Macdonald

illustrated by
Rahele Jomepour Bell

Albert Whitman & Co.
Chicago, Illinois

Me.

You.

One.

Two.

Stop.

Go.

Fast.

Slow.

Good.

Bad.

Happy.

Sad.

Old.

New.

Red.

Blue.

Eyes.

Nose.

Fingers.

Toes.

Table.

Chairs.

Window.

Stairs.

High.

Low.

Stay.

Go.